The DUCK Who Loved ICE CREAM

AuthorHouse™
1663 Liberty Drive
Bloomington, IN 47403
www.authorhouse.com
Phone: 1 (800) 839-8640

Because of the dynamic nature of the Internet, any web addresses or links contained in this
book may have changed since publication and may no longer be valid. The views expressed
in this work are solely those of the author and do not necessarily reflect the views of
the publisher, and the publisher hereby disclaims any responsibility for them.

ISBN: 978-1-7283-1419-8 (sc)
ISBN: 978-1-7283-1418-1 (e)

Library of Congress Control Number: 2019906753

This book is printed on acid-free paper.

Print information available on the last page.

Published by AuthorHouse 08/23/2019

The DUCK Who Loved ICE CREAM

CITY PARK

MARTIN LATIGUE

I am a duck who used to live in the city park. My name is Peachy.

Children visited the park, and sometimes they fed me.

One day, a kid was eating ice cream and dropped it on the ground. This was my first time eating ice cream. Since that day, I'd do anything for ice cream.

I started staying near the ice cream stand, watching the kids buy and eat ice cream, hoping that one of the kids would drop his or her ice cream.

In the summertime, Mark the policeman visited the park five or six times during the week. He always had ice cream, and sometimes he dropped it.

I walked behind him, following him as he was eating his ice cream. Mark noticed me walking behind him. When he ate the last bit of ice cream, I stopped following him. The next day Mark bought two ice creams, one for him and one for me.

He said, "I noticed you like ice cream. If you could talk, I would give you all the ice cream you could eat. I know you see and hear the criminal activities here in the park."

I had heard that an old duck in the city hall park could talk to people. He was smart and wise, and so I made the trip uptown to meet him. The trip took two days: ducks can't walk fast.

At the end of summer, I moved to the city hall park to winterize and learn how to talk from the old duck.

For the next six months, I practiced. After that, the time was right to let Mark know that I could talk. When I saw Mark coming into the park, I walked behind him and said, "Hello, Mark."

He just stood there looking at me.
Then he asked what I knew
about crimes in the park.

We became partners in fighting crime. I would walk up to the criminals as they talked about crimes. I would pass this information to Mark. We were able to stop crime in this park within six months. All the ducks in the park helped. They spied on criminals and passed the information on to me.

Mark and I moved to the city hall park, the place of the old duck, to fight crime. Mark let me ride in his car, which I enjoyed. It took us six months to clean up the crime in that park.

Mark received many awards and cash rewards. When he retired, he bought a farm and moved his family and me to the country.

I had not been to the country before—I was born in the city. At the farm, I met other animals. I didn't know that cows were so big, and my friend the old duck from the city hall park was there. At night he and I watched the sunset together and listened to the sounds of the crickets. They made high-pitched sounds, and the frogs made their sounds, too, to praise and glorify the Lord.

This story is about a duck who loves ice cream. The taste of ice cream was the driving force that made this duck want to talk for the rewards of ice cream.

Milk and cream contain natural sedatives that soothe the nervous system. Ice cream refreshes the body, helps with sleep, and cools you off on a hot day.

Is ice cream the Old Testament's milk and honey? It sure is heavenly.

You will enjoy this story more if you eat ice cream before reading. You will be grateful.

Printed in the United States
By Bookmasters